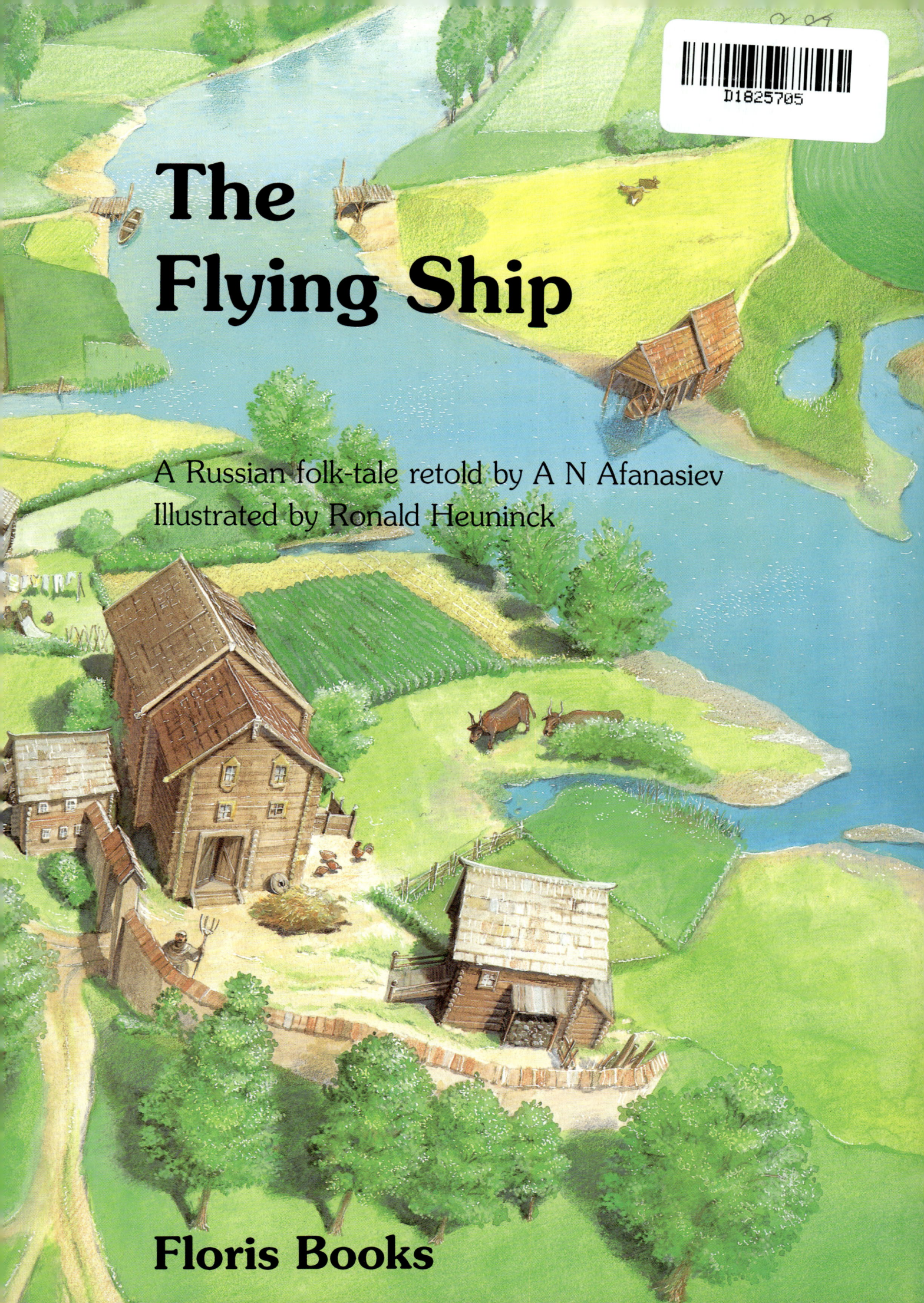

The Flying Ship

A Russian folk-tale retold by A N Afanasiev
Illustrated by Ronald Heuninck

Floris Books

Once a husband and wife had three sons; two were smart and good-looking, but the youngest was a little dull and slow, so they came to call him Simpleton.

The clever ones were pampered, and their mother fed them well and gave them a clean shirt every week. But mostly they just laughed at Simpleton, because he was so foolish.

Then one day came great news. The tsar had invited everyone to a huge feast, and promised his daughter's hand in marriage to any man who could build a ship that would fly.

The clever brothers talked this over eagerly. "We shall go to the palace," they said, "and surely make our fortune there."

Their parents begged them to stay at home, but the two of them declared, "We're going, and that's it! Give us your blessing and something for the journey."

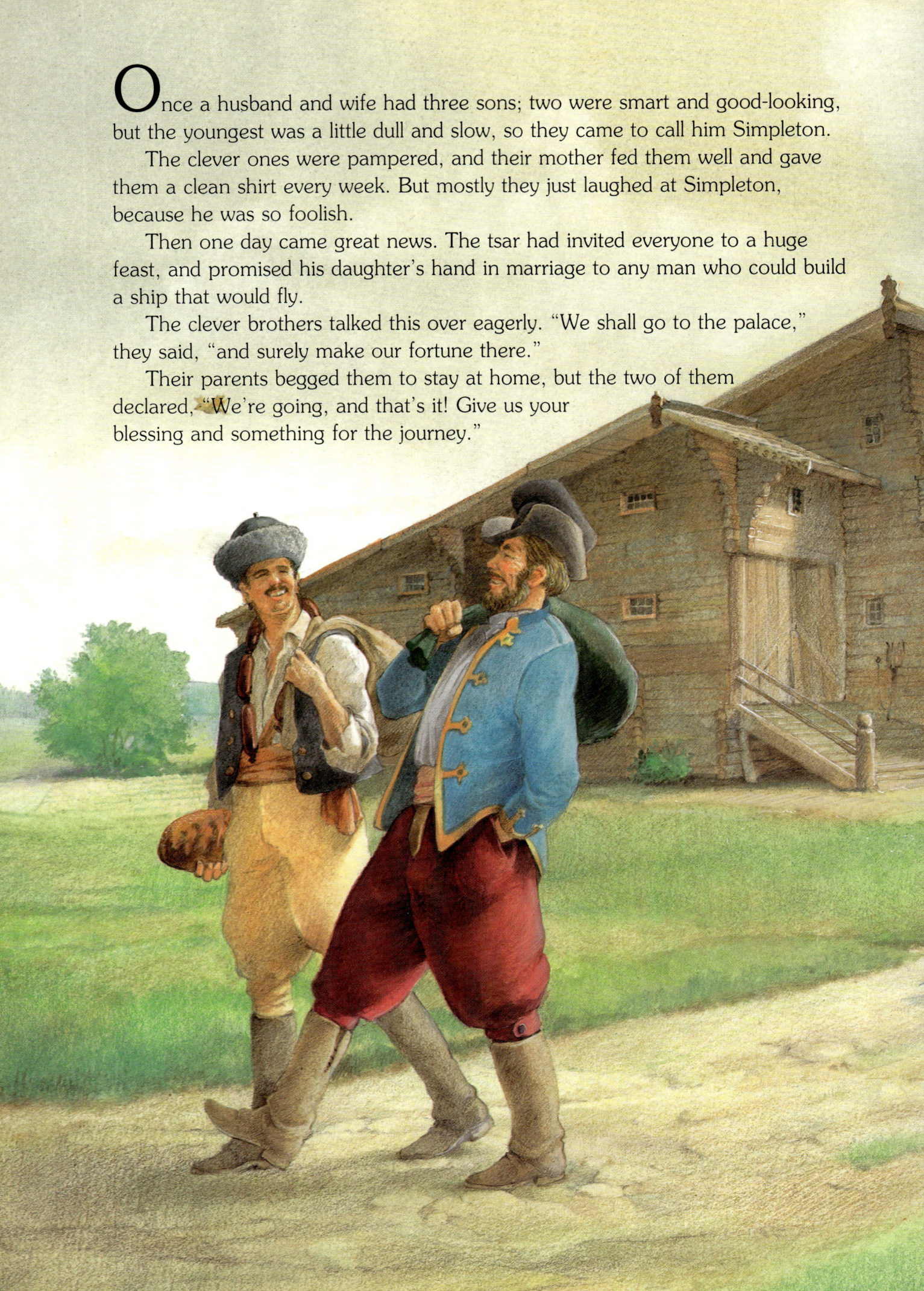

Their mother gave them white bread, cooked meat, and a bottle of schnapps, and off they went with their parents' blessing.

Seeing this, Simpleton said to his parents, "I want to go where my brothers have gone!"

"What are you thinking of, daft boy," said his mother, "the wolves will eat you."

"No, they won't," he answered. "I'm going."

His parents just laughed at him, but they couldn't change his mind. "All right then, go, if you must!" they said at last. "But please don't let on that you're our son!"

His mother gave him some stale black bread and a bottle of water, and saw him out of the house. And so Simpleton set off on his journey.

Simpleton wandered along and by the way met an old man with a white beard. "Where are you going, old man?" he asked.

"I travel about the world and help people in trouble. And where are you off to?"

"To the tsar's feast."

"Sit down," said the old man, "let's have a bite to eat. What have you got in that sack?"

"Only some stale old bread that you couldn't eat."

"Never mind, take it out."

Simpleton took it out, and the black bread had turned into the finest white wheaten-bread from a lord's table.

"Now," said the old man, "what are we going to drink?"

"I've only got water!" Simpleton brought the bottle out, only to find the water had turned into the finest vodka.

"See what God gives to simple folk!" said the old man, smiling.

They spread their coats on the grass, sat down, and made a good meal of it all. Then the old man thanked Simpleton and said: "Listen carefully. Go into the forest and give the first tree you see a blow with your axe. Then lie on the ground until someone wakes you up. He will have a flying ship for you. Get in and fly wherever you want, but be kind to those you meet on the way."

Simpleton thanked the old man and said goodbye. He walked into the forest, went up to the first tree, struck it with his axe, fell to the ground and went to sleep. After a while, he heard someone say: "Get up, your fortune's as good as made!"

Simpleton woke, and there was the flying ship, all of gold, with silken sails which filled and pulled as though they wanted to take off. He didn't hesitate but climbed up into the ship, which rose higher and higher and flew off.

The ship flew below the sky and above the earth, and the whole world spread out below as far as the eye could see.

After a while Simpleton saw a man lying in the road with one ear to the ground. He shouted to him: "What are you doing down there?"

"I'm listening to find out if the guests have arrived at the tsar's feast."

"Why, do you want to go there too?"

"Indeed I do!"

"Get in, I'll take you." So he got in and away they flew.

They flew on and on, and soon they saw a man hopping along with one leg strapped to his ear.

"Why are you hopping along on one leg?" they cried out.

"Because if I untied the other leg, each stride would take me right across the world."

"Get in with us and come to the tsar's feast."

"I will!" he replied. And he got in, and away they flew again.

They flew on and on, and there they saw a marksman taking aim with his gun, but with no target anywhere to be seen.

Simpleton called out: "What are you shooting at, when there's nothing in sight?"

"What do you mean? I'm shooting at a pigeon a hundred miles away."

"Come with us to the tsar's feast!" they said.

And he got in and away they flew.

They flew on and on, and very soon they saw a man walking along with a huge basket of bread on his back.

"Where are you going?"

"I'm going to get some bread for lunch," he replied.

"But you've already got a whole basketful!"

"That little scrap is just for a snack!"

"Get in and come to the tsar's feast!" they cried.

And he got in as well, and away they flew.

They flew on and on, and suddenly they saw a man standing by a lake as though he were looking for something.

"What are you looking for down there?"

"I'm looking for a decent drink of water."

"But there's a whole lakeful in front of you."

"That drop of water is barely a gulp for me."

"Then come along with us to the tsar's feast!"

He got in, and away they flew.

They flew on and on, and suddenly saw a man carrying a sheaf of straw.

"Where are you carrying that straw?" they asked.

"To the village," he replied.

"Isn't there enough straw in the village?"

"Ah, this is no ordinary straw. If it was as hot as could be, and you spread out this straw, there'd be frost and snow in an instant."

"Come with us to the tsar's feast!" they cried.

And he got in as well, and away they flew.

And they flew on and on, and suddenly saw a man walking with a bundle of twigs over his shoulder.

"Where are you carrying those twigs to?"

"To the forest."

"Aren't there plenty of twigs in the forest already?"

"Yes, but none like these," he replied. "If you scatter these twigs on the ground, they turn into soldiers."

"Get in and come to the tsar's feast!" they cried.

And he agreed to come, and away they flew.

They flew on for a long while, and in the end they arrived at the tsar's feast. Half the kingdom had gathered there: old men and young, of every rank and station, rich and poor. Tables were laid in every courtyard, and barrels of mead and vodka stood in rows. There was as much food and drink as you can imagine!

Simpleton and his new friends came sailing past the tsar's window, landed their ship and went off to eat. The tsar looked out in amazement and ordered a servant to find out who the golden ship belonged to.

Very soon the servant came back, saying: "It seems a crowd of ragged peasants arrived in the ship!"

The tsar didn't believe him. "How can a bunch of peasants have flown here in such a fine ship?" he said. So saying, he went down into the crowd himself, and asked: "Who flew here in that wonderful ship?"

Simpleton stepped forward and said: "It was I, your Majesty, sir."

The tsar was appalled to see patches on the boy's coat and holes in his trousers, and went back inside beating his forehead, saying to himself: "How can I possibly give my dearest child to this peasant?"

But what could he do to get out of his promise? He decided he must give the boy an impossible task to perform.

"Go to him," he told his servant, "and say if he wants my daughter's hand in marriage, he must fill a flask with healing water from the ends of the earth and bring it to me before the people have finished eating. And if he fails to fetch me the water in time, I'll have his head cut off."

The servant went down and delivered the tsar's command. Simpleton, on hearing this, became utterly miserable.

The runner saw this and asked him: "Why so sad?"

Simpleton told him the sorry news. "The tsar has said I must fetch him a flask of healing water from the ends of the earth before the people have finished eating. How can I possibly set about it?"

"Don't worry, I'll fetch it for you." So saying, the runner untied his leg from his ear, and with two strides he reached the ends of the earth and filled a flask with healing water. But as he was rather tired, he thought: "I can easily get back in time. I'll just sit down here and have a quick rest."

But it was such a warm day, he very soon fell fast asleep. Meanwhile, at the palace, the dinner was nearly over, but there was no sign of the runner. Simpleton sat waiting, more dead than alive. "I've had it!" he thought to himself. "I'm going to have my head cut off!"

But the listener put his ear to the ground, and he said: "The rascal's gone to sleep. I can hear him snoring!"

Then the marksman cried: "Don't worry! I'll wake him up!" And he aimed his gun and fired, and the shot struck the side of the mill, sending the splinters flying. The runner woke up with a start and hastened back just in time as the people were finishing their dinner.

What could the tsar do now? He set Simpleton a new task. "If he and his friends can eat six brace of roast oxen and all the bread from forty ovens, I'll give him my daughter for his wife. If he fails, I'll cut his head off!"

When Simpleton heard this, he began to weep. But the bread carrier said: "Don't cry! I'll eat the whole lot for you, and it'll only seem a little snack to me."

So the tsar's servants roasted twelve oxen and baked forty ovens full of bread. But when the bread carrier set to, not a single crumb was left, and all he said was: "That was a nice appetiser! If only they'd given me a decent meal!"

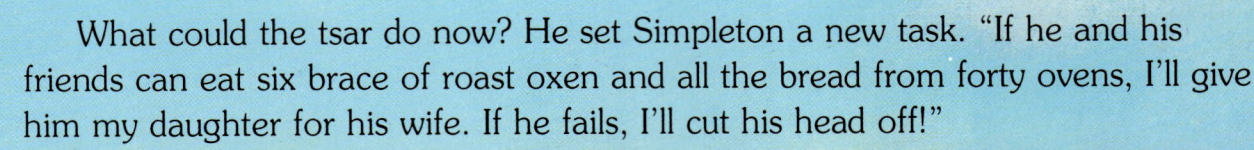

The tsar saw that Simpleton could do almost anything, and set him a new task. He and his friends had to drink forty barrels of water and forty barrels of wine after that. "And if he can't do it, I'll cut his head off!" declared the tsar.

Simpleton wept again at the size of the task. But the drinker said, "Don't cry. I'll drink the whole lot myself, and it will seem only a cupful to me."

So they brought forty barrels of water and forty barrels of wine. And when the drinker set to, not a single drop was left, and he laughed at them: "That wasn't very much! What a thirst you've left me with!"

When the tsar saw that he couldn't get the better of Simpleton, he thought: "I'll have to rid myself of this scoundrel or he will get my poor daughter into his clutches!"

He ordered the sauna to be heated until it was so hot that it would cook anyone inside. Then he sent his servant to Simpleton saying: "The tsar has said you must take a bath before your wedding."

But Simpleton was warned by the listener, who had heard the tsar's commands, and took the straw-carrier into the sauna with him. Soon after they went in, it grew so hot they could scarcely bear it. But the man spread out his straw and it turned so cold that Simpleton had to climb on the stove because he was chilled to the bone.

Early the next morning they opened the sauna, expecting to find only ashes in there. But Simpleton was lying asleep on the stove, and when they woke him he only said: "Ah, what a comfortable night I had!"

The tsar was very disturbed to hear all this. What now could be done with the peasant boy? He thought and thought, and had another idea.

"Very well," he said, "if he can produce a regiment of soldiers for me by tomorrow morning, I'll give him my daughter as his wife. But if he fails, I'll cut his head off!"

He laughed to himself. Where could a simple peasant get a regiment from in a day? Even he, the tsar, could scarcely manage it!

On hearing this latest task from the tsar, Simpleton went and said to his companions: "Help me once more, brothers! Otherwise it's goodbye to this world for me!"

"Don't worry," said the man who carried the twigs, "I'll save you all right."

That night, Simpleton's companion went into the fields, taking the bundle of twigs with him. And as he scattered them, each twig became a soldier, and very soon such an army gathered that it was impossible to count them!

Early the next day, the tsar woke and heard
music playing. He asked: "Who is playing so early
in the morning?"

They replied: "It's the man with the golden
ship, carrying out manoeuvres with his army. And
he says, if you don't give him your daughter now,
he'll take her by force."